LITTLE THUMB

ONCE UPON A TIME, THERE WAS A COUPLE OF WOODCUTTERS WHO HAD SEVEN CHILDREN. THE YOUNGEST WAS SO TINY THAT HE WAS CALLED LITTLE THUMB.

AS THEY WERE VERY POOR, THE PARENTS DECIDED TO ABANDON THE CHILDREN IN THE FOREST. THE YOUNGEST OVERHEARD THE CONVERSATION AND HAD THE IDEA TO COLLECT PEBBLES NEAR THEIR HOUSE. THE NEXT DAY, THEY ALL WENT OUT TO CUT WOOD IN THE FOREST.

AT THE MOMENT WHEN THE CHILDREN WERE DISTRACTED BY THEIR WORK, THE PARENTS LEFT. HOURS LATER, THE BOYS REALIZED THEY WERE ALONE.

LITTLE THUMB TOLD HIS SIBLINGS THAT HE HAD LEFT PEBBLES ALONG THE ROAD SO THEY WOULDN'T GET LOST. SO, THE BOYS WENT BACK HOME.

THE NEXT DAY, THE FAMILY RETURNED TO THE FOREST. SINCE HE COULDN'T FIND ANY MORE PEBBLES, LITTLE THUMB MARKED THE PATH WITH PIECES OF BREAD. HOWEVER, WHEN IT WAS TIME TO LEAVE, HE REALIZED THAT THERE WERE NO CRUMBS LEFT. THE SIBLINGS BECAME DESPERATE AND WALKED FOR HOURS UNTIL THEY FOUND A CASTLE. TIRED AND HUNGRY, THEY KNOCKED ON THE DOOR.

THE WOMAN WHO RECEIVED THEM SAID SHE WAS THE SISTER OF A GIANT WIZARD WHO LIKED TO EAT CHILDREN. HOWEVER, AS SHE FELT SORRY FOR THE BOYS, SHE DECIDED TO HIDE THEM IN THE CASTLE. BUT THE OGRE SMELLED THE BROTHERS AND WENT LOOKING FOR THEM.

WHEN HE FOUND THE BOYS, THE GIANT SAID THAT THE NEXT DAY THEY WOULD BE HIS LUNCH, LEAVING THEM DESPERATE.

SO, WHEN THE WICKED OGRE SLEPT, THE BOYS MANAGED TO ESCAPE WITHOUT HIM NOTICING.

UPON WAKING UP, THE OGRE SAW THAT THE BOYS WERE NO LONGER THERE. FURIOUS, HE PUT ON HIS MAGIC BOOTS, WHICH GAVE HIM MORE ENERGY, AND WENT AFTER THEM. WHEN HE REALIZED THAT THE GIANT WAS APPROACHING, LITTLE THUMB TOLD HIS BROTHERS TO KEEP WALKING AND HID BEHIND A TRE

WHEN THE WIZARD STOPPED TO REST AND SLEPT, THE LITTLE BOY TOOK OFF HIS MAGIC BOOTS.

SINCE HE WAS WITHOUT HIS MAGIC BOOTS, THE WICKED ONE RAN OUT OF ENERGY AND FELL INTO A DEEP SLEEP.

LITTLE THUMB PUT ON THE OGRE'S BOOTS, RETURNED TO THE CASTLE, AND TOLD THE WOMAN THAT HER BROTHER HAD BEEN CAPTURED BY BANDITS, AND THAT, TO PAY THE RANSOM, THE GIANT HAD ASKED HIM TO TAKE ALL THE GOLD HIDDEN IN THE CASTLE.

UPON SEEING THE LITTLE BOY WEARING HER BROTHER'S MAGIC BOOTS, THE WOMAN BELIEVED THE STORY AND HANDED OVER ALL THE TREASURE TO LITTLE THUMB. THEN, HE FOUND HIS BROTHERS AND TOGETHER THEY CONTINUED TO SEARCH FOR THE WAY HOME.

WHEN HE FINALLY ARRIVED HOME, LITTLE THUMB RAN INTO HIS PARENTS' ARMS AND SHOWED THEM ALL THE JEWELS HE HAD OBTAINED. THE FAMILY BECAME RICH, NEVER WENT HUNGRY AGAIN, AND BOUGHT A BIGGER HOUSE, WHERE THEY ALL LIVED HAPPILY EVER AFTER.

THE END.